ELEANOR JO
A Christmas to Remember

ELEANOR JO
A Christmas to Remember

ELEANOR CLARK

Dedication

To my grandchildren, and great grandchildren. May you recognize, love, and appreciate your rich Christian heritage and the privilege of living in America, which was founded on the trust and hope we have in Jesus. May you continue the legacy.

Contents

To my Lord and Savior, Jesus Christ, who has blessed me with the greatest family, life, and country. May every word bring honor and glory to Your name.

To my publisher, Jake Jones, who recognized the potential of my stories and my heart's desire to bless and encourage young readers to value their American and Christian heritage.

To my writer, Janice Thompson, who understood my love of history and breathed life into my stories with the skill of her pen.

After her grandmother turned off the light and closed the door, Holly leaned back against the soft, silky pillow and thought about Christmas. What fun they were going to have tomorrow morning—opening presents and listening to Grand Doll's story about the greatest gift of all. She could hardly wait.

CHRISTMAS HOLLY

*H*OLLY MARIE STOOD IN FRONT OF HER grandmother's Christmas tree and looked at the colorful ornaments. Each one had a special meaning. So did their colors of deep red and gold. She reached to touch a tiny crystal ornament in the shape of an angel. Something about it made her smile.

The sound of voices—her cousins, parents, aunts, uncles, and grandparents—rang out across the house. She loved that sound. In fact, she loved every single thing about Christmas—the presents, the food, the music. Everything. More than anything, though, she loved spending it with Grand Doll—her wonderful grandmother.

"Would you like to help me with the cocoa, Holly Marie?" Grand Doll's voice sounded from the kitchen.

"Yes ma'am." Holly let go of the little ornament and skipped across the living room, careful not to bump into her cousins along the way. When she arrived in the kitchen, she looked up at her grandmother, who was dressed in her special red Christmas dress, and smiled. "Merry Christmas, Grand Doll," she said as she reached up for a hug.

"Well, Merry Christmas to you, too, beautiful girl." Her grandmother wrapped her in a loving embrace. "Did you enjoy the Christmas Eve service tonight?"

"Mmmhmm." Holly nodded. "I love your church, and the music was so pretty."

"That's my favorite part too." Her grandmother looked into her eyes. "Christmas is the very best time of year, isn't it? And the music just makes it even better."

"Oh yes." Holly went to work, putting marshmallows in the colorful Christmas mugs Grandmother had purchased on her visit to Israel.

"It's no wonder you love this time of year." Grand Doll placed cookies on a tray as she talked. "You were named for this season. Every time I hear your name, I think of Christmas. You're our little Christmas Holly."

Holly couldn't help but giggle.

Grand Doll began to sing the Sans Day Carol, a song Holly knew quite well, one she never grew tired of hearing.

And Mary bore Jesus our Saviour for to be,
And the first tree in the greenwood, it was the holly.

Holly! Holly!
And the first tree in the greenwood, it was the holly!

On and on Grand Doll sang, her face bright with joy. Her beautiful white hair almost made her look like an angel—a little bit like the one on the tree, in fact. Holly stood in silence, just watching and listening with great anticipation.

Finally her grandmother finished singing. She looked at Holly with a warm smile as she spoke. "Did you know your mama was thinking of that song when she named you?"

"Yes ma'am." Holly nodded. She had heard the story many times but loved it every time.

"It's a wonderful song about the birth of our Savior," Grand Doll said. "Your name 'Holly' is a reminder to us all that God sent His Son into the world at Christmastime. It's a very special name for a very special girl."

Holly wrapped her arms around her grandmother's waist and whispered, "Thank you, Grand Doll. I love you!"

After a moment, her grandmother stepped back and looked at the tray filled with cookies and cocoa. "What do you think? Should we invite the others to our little party?"

"Yes, please!"

Grand Doll carried the tray into the living room and set it on the coffee table near the tree. "Time for hot chocolate and cookies, everyone," she called.

The room filled quickly, and everyone reached for the mugs and the large, warm sugar cookies. As the children sat down in front of the fireplace, Grand Doll and Poppie took their seats in the big leather chairs nearby. Holly's mother and father sat on the sofa. Holly squeezed down into the little spot between her parents—happy to be so close to the people she loved the most. Christmas music played softly in the background as they enjoyed the yummy sweets.

"Is everyone ready for Christmas?" Poppie asked, with a twinkle in his eye.

All of the children began to talk at once, and the room grew really noisy.

Holly's father laughed. "I know some boys and girls who aren't going to get much sleep tonight."

"I'll sleep. I promise!" Holly whispered in her mama's ear.

Her mother smiled and patted her on the leg. "That's my good girl."

Poppie took another cookie from the tray and winked at Grand Doll as he spoke to the others. "Your grandmother is the best cook in all of Texas."

Grand Doll's cheeks turned pink as she said, "My papa used to tell me I would be some day, but there will be plenty of time to decide that after Christmas dinner tomorrow."

Everyone started talking about the food they would enjoy the next day. All but Holly Marie. She sat quietly and sipped her hot chocolate, just listening. Sometimes listening was more fun than talking anyway. When she finished the cocoa, she set her mug down on the coffee table and curled up next to Mama, resting her head on her shoulder.

"Getting sleepy?" Mama asked.

"Mmmhmm."

The large evergreen tree next to the sofa smelled like cedar, which made Holly's nose tickle. She let out a sneeze. Everyone in the room said, "Bless you!" at the same time.

Holly giggled and then buried her face in her mother's arm, embarrassed. Soon her eyelids grew heavy, and she closed them just for a minute. A little while later, she felt someone lift her and carry her into the bedroom. She opened her eyes and looked up at her father. "Did I fall asleep?" she asked with a yawn.

"You did." He set her down on the edge of the bed and kissed her on the forehead.

Her mother followed them into the room to help Holly dress for bed. After that, her cousins Chelsea and Rachel burst in, talking, talking, and talking about Christmas. Before long, Holly was wide awake again.

A few minutes later, Grand Doll came into the room to turn off the light and kiss the girls goodnight. She sat on the edge of the bed and smiled at her granddaughters. "Are you excited about Christmas Day?" she asked.

"Yes!" Chelsea squealed as she bounced up and down on the bed. "Presents!"

"Tomorrow I'm going to tell you a story about a very special gift," Grand Doll said. "The very best one of all."

"What kind of gift?" Rachel asked.

"One that keeps giving and giving and giving," Grand Doll explained. "But right now, I see three granddaughters who need to get a good night's sleep. Just as soon as they say their prayers, that is."

They bowed their heads and prayed, and then Holly and the other girls climbed under the covers, giggling all the way. "Merry Christmas Eve, Grand Doll," they all chorused.

After her grandmother turned off the light and closed the door, Holly leaned back against the soft, silky pillow and thought about Christmas. What fun they were going to have tomorrow morning—opening presents and listening to Grand Doll's story about the greatest gift of all. She could hardly wait.

But she must wait. Her eyes were growing heavy. She let out a great big yawn. Before she knew it, Holly drifted off into Christmas dreamland.

It seemed like no time at all had passed before she awoke to the morning sunlight streaming in the window.

"It's Christmas!" Holly shouted the words as soon as her eyes opened. She looked across the bed at the other girls. Both were still asleep. "Wake up! Wake up!"

Chelsea and Rachel popped up in the bed.

"It's not morning yet." Chelsea rubbed her eyes.

"The sun is coming up. Look." Holly pointed at the window and then sprang from the bed. "C'mon. Let's go!"

The girls jumped out of bed and raced into the living room where all of the others were gathering. Excited voices rang out all across the room. Holly searched through the crowd until she saw her mother. She went right away to Mama's arms and gave her a hug. "Merry Christmas!"

"Merry Christmas to you, Holly Marie."

Mama began to sing the Sans Day Carol, and Holly joined in. Grand Doll took pictures of the children dressed in their Christmas pj's, and then Poppie clapped his hands to get everyone's attention.

"Time for the scavenger hunt," he said.

"How fun!" Holly loved playing this game.

Grandfather opened the first clue and read it out loud. "Merry Christmas, one and all," he read. "Follow these special clues until you find the reason for the season. Start by looking in a place filled with yummy delights."

"Yummy delights?" Rachel asked. "The refrigerator?"

The children ran into the kitchen and opened the refrigerator door, looking for clues. Nothing.

"Ooo, I know!" Holly squealed. "The cookie jar. It's filled with yummy delights!"

Sure enough, they found the next clue inside the cookie jar. This one read, "Christmas music is so much fun. To find the next clue you must run, run, run to the place where the music is hidden."

"The piano bench!" Chelsea shouted.

Off they all ran to the living room to open the piano bench. Inside, they found the next clue. This one led them to the dining room where they found a message hidden under the silver teapot. That one took them to the sun porch where they found another clue in the flowerpot.

Up and down, all around…all over the house they ran, until they finally ended up at the place where the game always ended—the manger on the fireplace mantle. There the children found the tiny wood-carved baby Jesus, lying in the manger.

They settled down on the floor, and Poppie read the Christmas story from the Bible—the story of how God sent His son to the earth to be born in a stable. Holly knew the story by heart, but she loved hearing it anyway. She mostly loved the part where Poppie's eyes would fill with tears as he talked about how much God loved each one of them.

Afterwards, Grand Doll held the tiny wooden baby up for all of them to see. "I promised to tell you a story about a gift that keeps on giving," she explained. "That gift is Jesus. God sent Him as a gift—a present—for each of us."

"Jesus is a present?" Chelsea looked a little confused as she asked the question.

"That's right," Poppie said. "He's God's gift to the world. He came as a baby in a manger, but He grew into a man. Even though He never did anything wrong, He chose to take the punishment for our mistakes, our sins."

"He died on a cross for the sins of the world," Grand Doll added. "When He did that, He gave us the very best gift of all—eternal life." She went on to tell them that anyone who asked Jesus into his or her heart would get to live forever in heaven with Him. Holly loved this part of the story best.

She looked at the little manger scene and smiled. Jesus really was the best gift of all.

"Now, do I see some children who are ready to open presents?" Grand Doll asked.

Holly and the other children spent some time opening gifts and then playing together. They had a wonderful time. After that, her grandmother asked them to come into the kitchen for breakfast. As they ate, she shared more stories with them.

"Remember how you followed the clues until you found the baby Jesus?" Grand Doll asked.

The children nodded.

"Did you know that our family has left clues behind too?" she said.

"What do you mean?" Holly asked.

"If you search carefully, you will learn a lot about where you have come from. One story will lead you to the next, and then the next. Before long, you will discover surprises about your parents, grandparents, and great-grandparents. You can learn how we have celebrated Christmas over the years. Once you learn the family's stories, you can pass them on to your children, and they can pass them on to their children. You can keep them going, just like that scavenger hunt."

Holly tried to think about what it would be like to be grown up with children, but she couldn't. She wouldn't be grown up for a million, zillion years.

"I love telling stories about when I was a little girl," Grand Doll said. "Christmas was a lot different back then."

"Didn't you have presents?" Rachel asked.

"A few," their grandmother explained. "But I grew up during the depression—a time when families didn't have a lot of money to spend on Christmas presents."

Chelsea's lips turned down in a pout. "That's sad," she said.

"To tell you the truth, my parents didn't have much money for a lot of things like toys, shoes, cars, or fancy clothes. Our Christmases were very, very different from the ones today."

"Please tell us, Grand Doll." Holly said. She wanted to know more about her grandmother's life as a little girl.

Grand Doll's face lit with excitement. "I could tell you a Christmas story that happened when I was just the age you are now," she said. "Eight years old. My story takes place on the dairy farm where I grew up, not far from here."

"Christmas on a farm?" Chelsea said. "Doesn't sound like much fun to me."

"Oh, it was fun all right." Grand Doll's eyes glistened. "In fact, I'm going to tell you about the very best Christmas of my life, the one where I learned that Jesus was the Savior of the world. Of course, I wasn't known as Grand Doll back then. I was just little Eleanor Jo."

"Eleanor Jo." Holly smiled as she thought about what Grand Doll must have looked like as a little girl. She couldn't wait to hear all about it.

"Listen carefully, everyone." Her grandmother leaned forward in her big rocking chair with a broad smile on her face. "Pay close attention, because I have a wonderful Christmas story to tell…"

*Eleanor Jo bowed her head, and her
mother began to pray. She prayed
for many people that cold December
night—for Papa and his work on the
farm. For each of the children, that
they would grow up to know and love
the Lord. For a family named the
Johnsons who lived down the street—
because they had no Papa to care for
them. And for the many people who
didn't know Jesus—the best gift of all.*

WAITING FOR CHRISTMAS

MEXIA, TEXAS 1939

ELEANOR JO PRESSED HER NOSE AGAINST the icy cold windowpane and peeked outside. The skies above were heavy with clouds, but she didn't mind a bit.

"Do you think it will snow tomorrow, Mama?" she asked.

"Perhaps." Her mother joined her at the window. "Your papa says it's going to be a very cold winter. Are you hoping for snow?"

"Oh yes!" Eleanor Jo clapped her hands together in glee. "Just in time for Christmas. I can't wait."

"You must wait one more week," her mother said with a smile. "But it will seem even longer if you spend every waking moment daydreaming about Christmas."

"Oh, I won't. I promise." Eleanor Jo pushed a strand of long, brown hair from her eyes.

"The days go by faster when we work hard," Mama reminded her.

"I know." Eleanor Jo shivered, pulling her sweater tighter as she turned away from the window. Tomorrow would be a wonderful day. The dairy farm would look beautiful covered in white snow. And with school dismissed for the holidays, she could run and play with her little brother and sister instead of tending to her lessons.

Eleanor Jo crossed the room to the fireplace, where she stood in front of the orange and red flames that were fiery enough to take the chill off 'ole man winter. She rubbed her hands together until she felt warm all over.

"It's so hard *not* to daydream, Mama," she confessed with a little giggle. "I just love Christmas. I love everything about it."

"Me too," her little sister Martha Ann added as she skipped over from the other side of the room. "I love the food and decorations best."

"Food!" their four-year-old brother James squealed.

"Singing Christmas carols at church is my favorite part," Eleanor Jo added. "And opening presents too."

At the word *presents*, a look of sadness came into her mother's eyes. Mama sat in the large wooden rocking chair without saying a word, but Eleanor Jo could tell something troubled her.

"Have we said something wrong?" Eleanor Jo asked.

"No, honey." Her mother shook her head. "You've only said the things that all children say at this time of year. But I need you to understand that times are very hard right now."

"I know, Mama." Eleanor Jo planted a kiss on her mother's cheek. She knew that many families in their little town didn't have enough food to eat or shoes to wear.

"We might not have a lot of presents this year," Mama continued, "but we will have a joyful time celebrating the birth of our Savior together as a family."

"But I *love* presents." Martha Ann pouted as she climbed into Mama's lap. "Won't there be any at all?"

"Don't worry, little one." Mama reached down to give her a hug and kissed her on the top of the head. "You have already been given the best present of all."

"I have?" Martha Ann's big brown eyes sparkled as she tried to guess.

"*Jesus* is the best gift," Eleanor Jo said with a nod. "Isn't that right?"

"Yes, that's right." Her mother reached to take her hand. "And I'm so proud of you for knowing that at such a young age."

"I'm not *so* young." Eleanor Jo stood up straight and tall. "I'm nearly nine."

"Yes, you are." Mama chuckled. "And acting more like a grown-up young lady every day. Before you know it, you'll be preparing meals and caring for little ones of your own."

Hearing that made Eleanor Jo want to act more grown up. She would try very, very hard not to daydream or behave childishly.

Mama rose from her seat quite suddenly as she looked at the Grandfather clock. "Oh, my, I need to get supper ready. Papa will be in from work soon, and he will be hungry. Would you girls like to help me in the kitchen?"

"Yes." Eleanor Jo followed behind her mother into the kitchen. Mama stood at the wood-burning pot-bellied stove, stirring a crock full of beef stew. Eleanor Jo and Martha Ann set the table. Their little brother James tugged at Mama's skirts as she worked.

"Sing, Mama!" he begged.

Right away, she began to sing "The First Noel." Eleanor Jo's heart grew quite happy as she listened. Nothing sounded as pretty as Mama's beautiful singing voice.

Soon all of the children joined in, and before they knew it they were joyfully singing other Christmas carols to pass the time while they worked together. Eleanor Jo tried hard *not* to daydream about Christmas, but singing "Silent Night" only made it harder.

As the sun dipped into the colorful evening sky, Papa appeared at the door. He looked very tired. Eleanor Jo ran to meet him as he came in. "Oh, Papa! I'm so glad you're here. We've fixed the best dinner for you."

"Have you now?" he asked as he pulled off his coat. "I knew I could count on my girls to fill my stomach with good food. The way to a man's heart is through his tummy."

Moments later, the family gathered around the table, and Papa, with his rich, loving tenor voice, prayed over the meal. Eleanor Jo loved the sound of his praying nearly as much as Mama's melodic singing.

The stew tasted so good, and Eleanor Jo ate until her tummy was full. As she did, Papa shared stories of his work on the farm. He told a funny story about one of their pigs, a cute little pink one that Martha Ann had named Delilah. And Papa's eyes twinkled as he shared another story about their stubborn old mule, Road-ee.

Eleanor Jo listened to every word. She loved Papa's stories. His face lit up with joy as he talked.

"We have much to be thankful for this Christmas," he said. "We're going to have the best dinner in Mexia, Texas."

"Muh-*hay*-uh, Texas!" James mimicked their father in childish voice.

Eleanor Jo couldn't help but smile at her little brother. She loved the funny-sounding name of their little town.

Papa nodded. "You should see the size of the ham in the smokehouse."

"Mmm, ham!" Martha Ann rubbed her tummy. "I love ham!"

"Love ham!" James echoed, bouncing in his seat.

Eleanor Jo giggled. She loved ham too, but wanted to act grown-up, not silly like her little brother and sister.

Mama tapped her spoon against her water glass and cleared her throat. "I have an announcement," she said.

"An announcement?" Papa's brow wrinkled. "What is it?"

"We've been invited to a Christmas party!"

"A party!" Eleanor Jo and Martha Ann squealed at the same time.

Papa looked up from his bowl of stew with a smile. "Really? Where?"

Mama's cheeks turned pink with joy. "Mrs. Urschel's house. Isn't that lovely?"

Eleanor Jo's eyes grew wide. She had wanted to visit Mrs. Urschel's house ever since moving to the farm. How many times had she stared at the large beautiful home and wondered what it must look like on the inside? Now she would finally get to see for herself.

Mama explained that the party would be held on Saturday night at six o'clock, and all of the children were invited. From that moment on, Eleanor Jo couldn't stop thinking about it. She spent the rest of the meal daydreaming, in fact.

After dinner, Mama called the children into her room to bathe in the big metal washtub, which she had filled with hot water from the stove. As she bathed, Eleanor Jo thought about what kind of bathtub Mrs. Urschel must have at her house. Probably a big one with real gold faucets. Perhaps she would get to see for herself, very soon.

After bathing, Eleanor Jo dressed in her warmest nightgown. Mama towel-dried her hair and put it in a French braid. Then Eleanor Jo climbed into the large feather bed she shared with her little sister. She pulled the quilt up under her chin and stared out of the window at the night sky, deep in thought.

"Let's say our prayers." Mama sat on the edge of the bed.

Eleanor Jo bowed her head, and her mother began to pray. She prayed for many people that cold December night—for Papa and his work on the farm. For each of the children, that they would grow up to know and love the Lord. For a family named the Johnsons who lived down the street—because they had no Papa to care for them. And for the many people who didn't know Jesus— the best gift of all.

As Eleanor Jo drifted off to sleep that night, she whispered one extra prayer—a secret one. "Please, Lord," she prayed. "Please let it snow tomorrow."

After that, she drifted off to sleep, dreaming of a white Christmas.

Something outside the window caught her eye. She ran over to take a look. A winter wonderland, prettier than anything she had ever seen, took her breath away.

LET IT SNOW!

$\mathcal{T}$HE NEXT MORNING, ELEANOR JO AWOKE to the sound of her father's singsongy voice. *"Wake up and spit on the rock. It ain't quite day, but it's four o'clock. I know you're tired and sleepy too, but honey, we've got work to do!"*

She usually loved Papa's made-up morning song but not this early. Eleanor Jo groaned as she rolled over in the feather bed. She pulled the homemade quilt up over her head to stay warm, and grumbled from underneath the covers. "Do we have to get up, Papa? It's still dark outside. And it's not even a school day."

"Out of bed, sleepyhead!" he said with a laugh. "Mama needs your help in the kitchen."

Eleanor Jo kicked back the covers and gave a little shiver. "Ooo, it's cold in here."

"You'll warm up just as soon as you get busy," he said.

The smell of bacon filled the little house, and Eleanor Jo's tummy rumbled. "Breakfast!"

"Mmm." Martha Ann yawned and stretched as she came awake. "Smells so good!"

As she dressed, Eleanor Jo thought about Mrs. Urschel and wondered what kind of breakfast she must be eating this morning in her big, fine house. Something fancy, perhaps? And surely she must eat on lovely china plates, not worn, chipped ones, like Eleanor Jo and her family had. "Must be wonderful," she whispered.

After dressing, Eleanor Jo went into the kitchen to help her mother set the table. Something outside the window caught her eye. She ran over to take a look. A winter wonderland, prettier than anything she had ever seen, took her breath away.

"Oh, how exciting! It snowed last night."

"I thought you'd never notice!" Her papa's voice rang out from behind her.

Eleanor Jo turned to face him. "Is that why you woke us up so early?"

"It is." He chuckled. "I know how much you love the snow, and I figured you wouldn't want to miss a minute of it. I imagine it will melt by afternoon, but that will give you children plenty of time to make snow angels after breakfast."

"Oh, Papa!" She couldn't hide her excitement. "I prayed for snow last night."

"Did you now?" he asked.

Eleanor Jo nodded. "I did. And God answered my prayers. There's nothing prettier in the whole wide world."

"I dare say, those big brown eyes of yours are a mite prettier than the snow," Papa said with a smile.

Eleanor Jo giggled and felt her cheeks warm in embarrassment. She loved it when Papa complimented her eyes.

Just then, Martha Ann entered the kitchen, still dressed in her nightgown, but with her snow boots sticking out from underneath. "Snow!" she squealed.

Mama placed a plate full of bacon on the table and then turned to give her a stern look. "Take off those snow boots, young lady. You won't be going outside till after breakfast."

"But, Mama, I need to use the outhouse." Martha Ann pouted.

"Ah. I see. Well, go on then. And Eleanor Jo, you might as well go with her to make sure she doesn't decide to run off and play."

Eleanor Jo nodded.

Mama smiled. "Just come back right away, you two, or your breakfast will be cold."

"Yes ma'am," both girls spoke together.

Eleanor Jo pulled on her snow boots and coat and then scooted out of the back door with her little sister at her side. As they headed off to the tiny outhouse just a few steps away, she heard Papa say, "One of these days we'll have an indoor bathroom. I promise."

But Eleanor Jo didn't mind. In fact, she had a wonderful time swishing through the fluttery mounds of snow to get to the tiny wood-framed outdoor bathroom. All along the way, she looked at the fields covered in white and daydreamed about the snow angels she and her sister would create later on that morning. What fun they would have together.

After finishing up outside, they headed back to the house, laughing and talking all the way. When they arrived back in the kitchen, Eleanor Jo and Martha Ann took off their boots and coats and joined Mama, Papa, and James at the table. Papa prayed over their meal, and then they started to eat.

"These biscuits are light as feathers, Mama!" Eleanor Jo said after biting into one. Nothing tasted better than Mama's homemade biscuits and homemade fig preserves, unless you counted the vanilla bean ice cream she made from snow. That was especially yummy.

Her mother's cheeks turned pink. "Light as feathers, eh? That sounds like something you've heard your father say."

Papa winked at Eleanor Jo. "No doubt your mama is the best cook in the whole county. Even Pastor Weathers says so. And half the neighbors."

"Oh, posh," Mama said. "That's not true."

"I only tell the truth." Papa gave another wink. "And the girls will surely agree."

Eleanor Jo nodded. "You are the best, Mama."

Papa smiled across the table at her and nodded. "One of these days you will cook like your mama."

Eleanor Jo sat up in her chair, proud as could be. "I can already make biscuits," she said. "I roll them out and cut them into circles, just like Mama."

Everyone began to talk about cooking—all but Papa, who told jokes and shared funny stories. When they finished eating, he poured a cup of coffee and leaned back in his chair, looking over the family.

"It might be snowing out, but there's still plenty of work to do," he said. "The hogs need to be fed, and someone needs to fetch the eggs from the henhouse."

"I'll get the eggs, Papa." Martha Ann offered.

Eleanor Jo drew in a deep breath. Feeding the hogs wasn't her favorite chore, but she would do it to help her father. Just when she started to speak, Papa interrupted.

"I'll tell you what…" He looked at them with a smile. "This morning I do believe I can take care of the chores myself so you children can play. How would that be?"

"Really?"

"Really. It's almost Christmas, and I want you children to enjoy your holiday. And besides, feeding the hogs is something I enjoy."

"You do?" Eleanor Jo stared at him, not quite believing her ears. How could anyone enjoy feeding pigs?

"Sure." His eyes sparkled as he talked. "The Bible says we should do everything 'as unto the Lord,' and I suppose that means feeding the hogs too. A good attitude will take you a long way when there's work to be done. Makes the chores much easier."

Eleanor Jo sighed as she listened to her father. He was such a wise man, and he knew so much about the Bible. Maybe one day she would know as much as her papa.

After breakfast, she and her sister helped Mama tidy up the kitchen. Then they bundled up in their coats and boots to play outside. Eleanor Jo raced across the white field, feeling a little bit like an angel bouncing across the clouds in the sky above.

"Catch me if you can!" she called out to Martha Ann. But, of course, her little sister could not catch up, so Eleanor Jo slowed down and waited.

Soon enough the two of them found a smooth patch of snow and lay down side by side. They moved their arms and legs back and forth in the white fluff to create spots that looked like angel's wings. Then, when they were done, they rested there a moment longer in silence. Finally both girls stood and stared at the marks they had made.

"Do you think the angels up in heaven look like *our* angels?" Martha Ann asked.

"I don't know." Eleanor Jo shrugged. She tried to imagine what they must look like.

"These are special Christmas angels." Martha Ann giggled.

Eleanor Jo pulled her coat a little tighter and thought about that for a moment. "There really *were* Christmas angels," she explained. "Real ones."

"There were?" Her little sister's eyes grew quite large.

"Yes." Eleanor Jo remembered a story Pastor Weathers had read from the Bible last Sunday morning. "The Christmas angels appeared to the shepherds and told them that baby Jesus had been born in Bethlehem. The angels sang, 'Glory to God in the highest!'"

"Glory to God in the highest," Martha Ann echoed.

For some reason, Eleanor Jo felt like stretching out in the snow one last time. She lay there shivering for just a moment before she started moving her arms and legs up and down, up and down.

As she created fresh angel wings in the snow, the words, "Glory to God in the highest," sprang from her lips. Before long, Martha Ann joined her. Together, the two sisters sang praises to God as they left their markings in the snow.

———⇒❧⇐———

"I think it would be lovely to decorate the house for Christmas," Mama said with a twinkle in her eye. "And I have just the thing." She pulled out some bright red streamers and a big accordion bell.

———⇒❧⇐———

DECORATING FOR
CHRISTMAS

ATER THAT MORNING THE SNOW BEGAN TO melt just as Papa had said it would. It left little icy puddles all over the farm. Eleanor Jo's dog, Buster, pounced on the muddy stuff and barked in delight.

All morning long Eleanor Jo and Martha Ann ran and played and had a wonderful time together. They also helped Papa cut down a large cedar tree, which he carried into the house and placed in the living room. They followed closely on his heels.

Once the tree was in place, the girls removed their soggy coats. Underneath, their clothes were damp and dirty from rolling around in the melting snow.

Their little brother James laughed when he saw them. "You're all wet!" he cried out.

"Yes, you are," Mama observed. "And goodness gracious, your cheeks are pink, girls. Are you cold to the bone?"

"Cold to the bone," James echoed with a childish giggle.

"Mmmhmm," Eleanor Jo said, and she patted her little brother on the head. She shivered underneath the wet dress.

"M…m…me too!" Martha Ann's teeth chattered so loudly that you could hear them from across the room.

Eleanor Jo couldn't help but laugh at her little sister. She looked so cute with her curly hair all messy and her cheeks nice and rosy. But her dress didn't look so cute. In fact, Mama might just scold them when she saw how dirty their clothes were.

Instead of scolding, Mama helped the girls change clothes, and then she fed the family a nice, warm lunch— big hot bowls of leftover beef stew. Eleanor Jo ate every bite and even asked for more. Playing in the snow could make you quite hungry.

After lunch, Papa went back outside to work, and Mama made an announcement. "How would my girls like to do something fun to celebrate this special season?"

"What, Mama?" Eleanor Jo asked. Perhaps Mama wanted to bake tea cakes. Eleanor Jo loved helping her mother bake cookies.

"I think it would be lovely to decorate the house for Christmas," Mama said with a twinkle in her eye. "And I have just the thing." She pulled out some bright red streamers and a big accordion bell.

Martha Ann began to clap her hands. "Pretty, pretty!" she said.

"Where should we start?" Mama asked.

They hung the beautiful red streamers all over the living room, and before they knew it, the whole place looked festive and bright.

"Oh, I can hardly wait for Christmas," Eleanor Jo said with a giggle. "What fun we'll have."

Mama took a piece of a leftover streamer and fashioned it into a bow and set it on James's head. The girls giggled merrily.

"He's our little Christmas present," Mama said with a smile.

When they finished decorating, Eleanor Jo looked across the room at the cedar tree she and Martha Ann had helped Papa cut down just this morning after playing in the snow. It looked quite bare. No decorations. No star. Nothing. Just a lonely tree, sitting in the corner of the living room.

Mama joined her, and they looked at it together in silence for a moment.

"That tree could do with some decorating too, don't you think?" Mama crossed her arms as if deep in thought.

"Oh yes!" Eleanor Jo said.

"I have just the thing." Mama walked into the kitchen. Both of the girls followed along on her heels, wondering what she would do. "Eleanor Jo, would you fetch the popping corn from the cupboard?"

Eleanor Jo skipped off to the kitchen and searched for the corn. She couldn't find it right away and went on a search for it. She finally located it in the cabinet under the sink. She also found something else—a large basket of fruit. Mama must be hiding this for Christmas day. How fun! But she wouldn't spoil the surprise.

Eleanor Jo reached for the container that held the tiny hard kernels of corn and turned to face the others, holding it aloft.

"Ooo, popcorn!" Martha Anne squealed.

"Mmm, yummy!" James added.

"Remember, this corn will be for stringing, not eating," Mama said with a wink as she went to work.

Eleanor Jo nodded, but she really knew better. She knew Mama would let them eat a few pieces along the way.

Together, they used an old-fashioned popcorn popper—a rectangular metal box with a sliding lid, mounted on a long handle. It was long enough to hold over the fire in the fireplace where they popped the corn.

Before long, the room was filled with the wonderful smell of hot corn and the *pop, pop, popping* sound of kernels bouncing around in the popper. Something about that sound made Eleanor Jo think of Christmas.

All day long she had tried not to daydream, but she now found herself thinking about what Christmas would be like this year. Would there be any presents under the tree at all?

Well, no time to worry about such things now, not with so much work to be done! Mama put the bowl of popcorn on the kitchen table, and the girls went to work with needles and thread to string the white fluffy pieces together for the tree. Eleanor Jo nibbled away at the hot kernels of corn, eating nearly as many as she strung together.

"Ouchy, ouch!" Martha Ann said, holding up her finger. "I poked myself!"

Mama kissed it and made it all better.

Eleanor Jo giggled. With the streamers all around the room and the long strands of popcorn, the whole house was really starting to feel like Christmas. She thought about Mrs. Urschel and tried to imagine what sort of Christmas decorations her large, beautiful house must hold, what special Christmas treasures. Would there be a lovely tree with fancy ornaments? Would she have red streamers too?

As soon as they finished a couple of long strands of popcorn, it was time to put them on the tree. Round and round Eleanor Jo and Martha Ann went, till the tree suddenly looked quite beautiful. After that, the children cut out shapes from colorful paper and crafted them into handmade decorations. Finally Mama cut out a star from bright gold paper and placed it atop the tree. They all stepped back to examine their handiwork.

"Ooo, beautiful!" Martha Ann said.

Eleanor Jo couldn't say anything. She couldn't stop staring at the pretty tree. How could a few strands of popcorn and homemade ornaments make such a big difference?

Mama glanced up at the clock on the way to the kitchen. "It's nearly three o'clock," she said. "I think we have just enough time for one more Christmas project before starting dinner."

"What's that, Mama?" Martha Ann asked, her little eyes gleaming with joy.

"How about some tea cakes to take to Mrs. Urschel's party?" Mama looked at the girls with a smile.

"Ooo, Mama! I was hoping you would say that. I love, love, love them!" Eleanor Jo bounced up and down.

"I know you do. And I love them too. But these will need to be extra-special ones, decorated with icing. Can you girls help me with that part?" Mama put on her most serious face.

"Oh yes," Eleanor Jo answered. She would decorate the prettiest tea cakes ever. Mama would be so proud and so would Papa. They would take the tea cakes to Mrs. Urschel's house for the big party, and all of the people in their town would see what a wonderful cookie-decorator she was.

After putting James down for a nap, they all went into the kitchen. Mama pulled out the large bin of flour and the smaller bin that contained white sugar crystals. She mixed up some eggs and butter, along with a little bit of vanilla extract, and then added sugar to the creamy mixture. Eleanor Jo watched carefully with her mouth watering. One day she would bake tea cakes for her children too. She just knew it.

Martha Ann tried to stick her finger in the bowl when Mama wasn't looking, but she got caught. She pulled back her hand with a sigh.

"I just wanted a nibble," she said.

"There will be plenty to eat when they're done," Mama scolded.

She added the flour to the mixture, along with some baking soda. Before long, the bowl was filled with the creamy white dough. Mama rolled it out onto waxed paper and handed cookie cutters to the girls. Eleanor Jo took one in the shape of a star and began cutting out cookies from the rolled dough.

Martha Ann's cookie cutter was in the shape of a little angel, but her cookies didn't look exactly like angels by the time she was done cutting them. Eleanor Jo didn't say anything. After all, Martha Ann was only six years old. She would get better with time. They placed the cookies in the pot-bellied stove, and before long, the kitchen filled with the sweet aroma of fresh-baked tea cakes. After they cooled, the real fun began. Mama made some icing out of powered sugar, butter, and milk, and let the girls decorate the little stars and angels. Eleanor Jo couldn't remember ever having such fun.

"Can we eat just one?" Martha Ann begged.

Eleanor Jo waited for Mama's response. The cookies were for the party at Mrs. Urschel's house. What would Mama say?

"I'll tell you what..." Mama looked up with a smile. "You can each have one after supper for dessert. How would that be?"

"Cookies!" James appeared in the kitchen doorway, his hair all mussed from his nap. "I love cookies!"

Mama gave him a kiss on the forehead, and then quickly got to work fixing supper. Before long, Papa came in from working outside. He looked extra tired.

Eleanor Jo ran to greet him. "Oh, Papa! What a fun day we had. We baked and decorated cookies, and put popcorn and decorations on the tree!"

His lips turned up in a big smile. "I thought I smelled popcorn," he said. "And the house looks so Christmas-y. Very nice!"

Eleanor Jo reached to give him one more hug before they sat together at the table for supper. "Thank you, Papa," she whispered.

"Thank you for what?"

"For doing our chores for us," she said. "So that we could have the best day ever!"

"Oh, that." He gave a little wave of his hand. "I had a fabulous time talking to the Lord while I worked. And I'm happy to hear you had a wonderful day."

Eleanor Jo thought about it as she ate her food. It *had* been a wonderful day. She had loved everything—from making snow angels to baking cookies. But as fun as it was, she couldn't help but think that tomorrow would be even more fun, for tomorrow they would attend the Christmas party at Mrs. Urschel's house. What a joyous time they would have!

———⟫●⟪———

Eleanor Jo put on her very favorite dress, made with Christmas red fabric and a white pique collar with red apples. She usually wore this dress to church on Sundays and for special occasions, of course. Tonight's party was a very special occasion.

———⟫●⟪———

THE CHRISTMAS
PARTY

*T*HE FOLLOWING DAY MAMA RUSHED around getting everyone dressed for the big party at Mrs. Urschel's house. "I want all of you to look clean and pressed," she said with a smile. "And be on your best behavior."

"We will, Mama," they all agreed.

Eleanor Jo put on her very favorite dress, made with Christmas red fabric and a white pique collar with red apples. She usually wore this dress to church on Sundays and for special occasions, of course. Tonight's party was a very special occasion.

Mama came into the room to fix her hair. Eleanor Jo sat on the chair in front of the mirror while Mama took out the rag curlers.

"Ooo," Martha Ann said, as she looked on. "You're curly-headed, Eleanor Jo!"

Eleanor Jo smiled at her reflection in the mirror. "I am," she whispered. In truth, she loved the long rings of curls. They almost made her look like a grown lady. Almost.

After finishing with her hair, Mama turned her attention to Martha Ann, who had somehow managed to smudge up her face and hands. "I can't turn my back on you for a second, young lady." Mama sighed and wiped her clean with a washcloth.

Eleanor Jo helped her mother by dressing James. She helped him put on his carefully pressed trousers and a button-up-the-front shirt. Then she slicked back his brown hair and stepped back to give him a glance.

"You look very handsome," she said.

James pulled at his shirttail. "Don't like this shirt," he grumbled.

Eleanor Jo shook her head in a motherly fashion. "I'm afraid you have to wear it, whether you like it or not. We're going to a party. A very fancy party. We must look our best."

"Papa, do I have to go?" James called out as he ran across the house to find their father.

Soon Papa appeared. He looked so handsome in his Sunday pants and crisp, clean shirt that he almost took Eleanor Jo's breath away.

"Papa!" she exclaimed.

"Well, don't you look pretty!" He swept her up into his arms and spun her around the room. "I dare say you'll be the belle of the ball at Mrs. Urschel's house."

Eleanor Jo felt her cheeks warm in embarrassment. "Thank you, Papa." She reached to give him a warm hug before he set her back down on the ground.

Soon Mama and Martha Ann joined them in the living room. Martha Ann's face had been spit-shined, and Mama looked beautiful in her dark blue dress.

Papa let out a little whistle. "Well, if you aren't a sight!" he said.

Mama's cheeks flushed. "Hush now, honey. You'll embarrass me in front of the children."

He gave her a wink in return, and then Papa placed the wide-brimmed Stetson on his head and turned to face the others. "Are we almost ready?"

Mama put on her hat and studied her reflection in the hallway mirror. Eleanor Jo couldn't help but think that Mama had the prettiest eyes in the county. They were big and brown and filled with love.

Martha Ann and James scrambled into their winter coats. Eleanor Jo slipped on her brown plaid coat and hat, and minutes later they were all on their way, driving to Mrs. Urschel's house in the family's big black Model A Ford.

"How far, Papa? How far?" Martha Ann begged.

"About five miles or so," he answered. "But it will seem longer if you talk about it the whole time."

Eleanor Jo didn't feel like talking. She wanted to enjoy the ride in silence, listening only to her imagination.

What would the house be like? Would Mrs. Urschel treat her kindly? Who else would attend the party? Would they all feel welcome?

Finally the moment came. The family pulled up in front of the elegant white house with large white columns on the spacious front porch. The railing of the porch was draped in cedar greenery, and the windows of the house were lit with candles. On the front door, a large wreath with a big red bow greeted them. The whole sight nearly took Eleanor Jo's breath away.

"Oh, Papa," she whispered, "it's even prettier up close."

With great excitement, the family parked the car and headed up the steps to the front door. Mama held the tray of cookies in her hand. Eleanor Jo couldn't stop staring at the large wreath, with its pinecones and red velvet bow. It was the prettiest thing she had ever seen.

Papa rang the bell, and they all held their breath until Mrs. Urschel answered.

"Welcome, neighbors!" A broad smile lit up her face. "I'm so happy you could make it. Please, come on in."

Eleanor Jo followed along behind Mama, not saying a word. She peeked around the edges of her mother's dress, trying to take in the beauty of the home. The inside was even nicer than the outside. The rooms were filled with elegant furniture, the most beautiful that Eleanor Jo had ever seen. The walls were covered with colorful pictures, and the dining table was covered in the prettiest china dishes Eleanor Jo had ever laid eyes on.

And the Christmas decorations! Eleanor Jo didn't know when she had ever seen such finery. Red velvet bows lined the stair railing, and boughs of evergreen hung draped about, making the room very colorful. And the whole place smelled like Christmas. Eleanor Jo took a deep breath, enjoying the fragrance.

"You have such a lovely home, Mrs. Urschel," Mama said.

"Please, call me Ruby Lee." The kindhearted lady gave her a hug. "I want you to feel at home in my house."

Eleanor Jo wondered if she could ever feel at home in such a grand place. It felt like a palace, or even a castle. Did people really live with such fine things—chandeliers, artwork, fancy dishes, and such? She couldn't imagine what it must feel like to have such luxuries.

When they arrived in the living room to greet the other guests, the huge Christmas tree came into view. Eleanor Jo could smell its fresh cedar scent.

Martha Ann gasped. "Oh, it's beautiful!"

The magnificent tree filled a corner of the room. The decorations were hand-painted, and brilliant in color. Candy canes covered the tree. Eleanor Jo licked her lips, just thinking about them.

"Oh, Mrs. Urschel," she said in a dreamy voice. "It's the prettiest tree in the world."

"Do you think so, honey?" The older woman gave the tree another glance. "I like it."

"Oh yes." Eleanor Jo couldn't think of another word to say, so she just stood, staring at the tree. She knew she shouldn't be jealous, but oh what fun it would be to have one like that.

"Do you have a Christmas tree at your house?" Mrs. Urschel asked them.

Martha Ann nodded. "Our tree is *so* pretty. And we strung popcorn to put on it."

Mrs. Urschel nodded. "I remember when I was just a girl. My mama popped corn, and we strung it to put on the Christmas tree. What a lovely tradition."

Soon the sounds of other people talking and laughing filled the room. More neighbors came in, and before long, people were singing Christmas carols, nibbling on sugar cookies, and sipping mugs of hot chocolate. Eleanor Jo loved every single minute, especially the part where the parents laughed and talked while taking bites of the yummy snacks on the dining room table.

Finally, when the others were busy talking, she took a moment to look around the house one more time. Everything was so beautiful, so…perfect. She found herself trying not to be envious, but it was a little hard. She strolled through several rooms before she finally stumbled across the indoor bathroom. Just as she had imagined, it was large and beautiful. And the faucets were, indeed, gold.

"How pretty!" she whispered, reaching to give one a touch. She was tempted to turn it on, to give it a try, but a voice from the other room caused her to pull back.

"Eleanor Jo," Mrs. Urschel hollered out from the living room, "You'd better come quick. We're about to sing 'Silent Night.' And I hear you have a lovely singing voice."

Eleanor Jo went back into the room and joined the others in the most wonderful Christmas carol of all. All the way through it, she thought about Jesus and what He must have looked like as a baby. He wasn't born in a big, fancy house like this one. He was born in a stable surrounded by cows and horses. No, He didn't live in a grand house back then, but Pastor Weathers said that everyone who loved and followed Jesus would one day live in heaven in mansions and walk on streets of gold. Eleanor Jo loved the Christmas story best of all.

After a great deal of time laughing, talking, and eating, it was time to leave. "We had such a wonderful time," Eleanor Jo's mother said as she gripped Mrs. Urschel's hand. "I can't tell you how lovely this home is, or how thankful we are to have been invited."

"Thank you all for coming." Mrs. Urschel looked at the children. "Now I'd like each of you to take something special to remember me by." She nodded her head toward the tree. Surely she didn't mean….

"Take a candy cane, children," Mrs. Urschel said. "And have a merry Christmas and a happy new year."

"Merry Christmas to everyone!" Martha Ann hollered out as she and James reached out to snag a candy cane from the tree. Eleanor Jo followed their lead, taking one for herself.

"I hope you all have a blessed and happy holiday season," Mrs. Urschel said with a smile. "And thank you for coming. We had a wonderful time."

As they headed back to the car, Eleanor Jo thought about the house—the front porch with the big white columns, the beautiful rooms inside with fancy furniture, and the artwork…everything. By the time they arrived back at their car, there was no doubt in her mind that coming to tonight's party was a little bit like getting a surprise Christmas present. What fun! And what a special treat.

Eleanor Jo and the others stood up and shouted out: "Glory to God in the highest, and on earth peace, good will toward men." Her heart flooded with joy as the words were spoken, for in that moment, she really was praising God for sending His Son into the world.

THE CHRISTMAS
PAGEANT

*T*HE DAY AFTER MRS. URSCHEL'S BIG party was Sunday, but not just any Sunday. This Sunday Eleanor Jo, along with her little brother and sister, would participate in a Christmas play at their church during the evening service. How special, to celebrate the real story of Christmas through singing and acting!

Papa drove the family to church just as the sun dipped into the western sky, and they sang Christmas carols the whole way. Eleanor Jo still couldn't stop thinking about the candy cane she had eaten the night before. What a tasty treat!

When they arrived at church, Mama helped the children into their angel costumes. Each child had a white robe and a tiny silver halo. All of the children chattered merrily as they prepared for the big event. After they were all ready, Mama clapped her hands together to get everyone's attention.

"After the congregation sings 'The First Noel' and 'It Came Upon a Midnight Clear,' you children will enter the sanctuary," she explained. "You will say, 'Glory to God in the highest, and on earth peace, good will toward men!' Make sure you say it loudly, with great joy in your voices."

Glory to God in the highest, and on earth, peace, good will toward men.

Eleanor Jo repeated the words to herself under her breath. They were the very same words she and Martha Ann had said as they made snow angels together. She looked over at her little sister and winked. Martha Ann winked back.

"After that," Mama continued, "you children will sit on the edges of the stage while I read the Christmas story from the gospel of Luke. Don't forget your line in the middle. Then all of you little angels will join together to sing "Hark the Herald Angels Sing" as you leave the sanctuary and return to the classroom."

Mary Lou Conner raised her hand. "Mrs. Bozeman?"

"Yes, dear?"

"This halo keeps falling off of my head."

Mama walked over and helped her fasten the glistening halo to her hair, and then she turned to face the others. "Should we pray before we begin?"

"Yes ma'am," they all said together.

Mama bowed her head and prayed that their performance would go well. She also prayed that people who might not know the Lord would come to know Him through their presentation. Eleanor Jo said a soft "amen" as the prayer ended.

Outside of the classroom, the organ sounded, and Eleanor Jo knew the service had begun. She waited in silence with the others for the congregation to finish singing. Finally the big moment arrived. She and the other children filed into the sanctuary and hollered out, "Glory to God in the highest, and on earth, peace, good will toward men!"

At that moment, Eleanor Jo looked over at Bucky Peterson, a ten-year-old boy known to be a prankster. He looked a little out of place in an angel costume to be sure. He pulled at the collar of his robe with a scowl on his face.

The children settled down on the edge of the stage while Eleanor Jo's mama read the story she loved so well from Luke, chapter 2.

"And it came to pass," Mama read, "in those days, that there went out a decree from Caesar Augustus, that all the world should be taxed. And all went to be taxed, every one into his own city. And Joseph also went up from Galilee, out of the city of Nazareth, into Judaea, unto the city of David, which is called Bethlehem; (because he was of the house and lineage of David:) to be taxed with Mary his espoused wife, being great with child.

Eleanor Jo thought about what Mama was reading. How could Mary ride on a donkey all the way to Bethlehem when she was expecting a baby? Must've been mighty uncomfortable. When Mama was expecting James, she couldn't have gone on a donkey ride. No way.

"And so it was, that, while they were there, the days were accomplished that she should be delivered." At this point, Mama's eyes grew quite large, and her voice grew very excited. Eleanor Jo leaned in to hear the next part.

"And she brought forth her firstborn son, and wrapped him in swaddling clothes, and laid him in a manger; because there was no room for them in the inn."

No room in the inn? That's why Jesus was born in a stable! Eleanor Jo thought to herself.

Mama continued on: "And there were in the same country shepherds abiding in the field, keeping watch over their flock by night. And, lo, the angel of the Lord came upon them, and the glory of the Lord shone round about them: and they were sore afraid. And the angel said unto them…."

At this point, Mary Lou Conner stood up and quoted the next line: "Fear not: for, behold, I bring you good tidings of great joy, which shall be to all people. For unto you is born this day in the city of David a Saviour, which is Christ the Lord. And this shall be a sign unto you; ye shall find the babe wrapped in swaddling clothes, lying in a manger."

Mama's voice began to shake with excitement as she read the next part. "And suddenly there was with the angel a multitude of the heavenly host praising God, and saying…"

Eleanor Jo and the others stood up and shouted out: "Glory to God in the highest, and on earth peace, good will toward men." Her heart flooded with joy as the words were spoken, for in that moment, she really was praising God for sending His Son into the world.

Mama smiled as the children took their seats once more. "And it came to pass," she continued, "as the angels were gone away from them into heaven, the shepherds said one to another, Let us now go even unto Bethlehem, and see this thing which is come to pass, which the Lord hath made known unto us. And they came with haste, and found Mary, and Joseph, and the babe lying in a manger."

Eleanor Jo closed her eyes for a moment and tried to picture what the stable must have looked like. Nothing like the big, fancy house she had been in the night before. And nothing like her own home, either. No, the place where Jesus had been born was probably a stinky, smelly place, filled with all sorts of animals—donkeys, horses, and the like.

When she opened her eyes, she looked across the stage and noticed Bucky listening closely. His scowl had disappeared, and a smile appeared in its place. Perhaps he wasn't such a prankster at Christmastime. And perhaps he was enjoying this story as much as she was.

Mama finished up the Christmas message with flair: "And when they had seen it, they made known abroad the saying which was told them concerning this child. And all they that heard it wondered at those things which were told them by the shepherds. But Mary kept all these things, and pondered them in her heart. And the shepherds returned, glorifying and praising God for all the things that they had heard and seen, as it was told unto them."

At this point, all of the little angels stood to their feet. Mrs. Conner, the church organist, began to play the introduction to "Hark, the Herald Angels Sing," and Eleanor Jo was swept away in the joy of singing about the birth of the Savior. On and on she sang with the other children, waiting for the moment to arrive where she would sing the solo.

In the very middle of the song, the others stopped singing as Eleanor Jo's voice rang out on the chorus— all alone. How wonderful, to sing such a heavenly song! And what a privilege to sing the big solo. Her voice shook a little, but not enough for anyone to notice...she hoped.

When she finished, the members of the congregation clapped, and she felt her cheeks get warm. She flashed a big smile at Papa, who sat on the second row looking very proud. And the look on Mama's face made her heart sing.

After the evening service ended, church members gathered for a time of refreshment. They served hot chocolate, hot apple cider with cinnamon sticks, and popcorn balls. The children ran and played and had a wonderful time

All but Eleanor Jo. She walked back into the sanctuary alone to think about the story her mama had read. She sat on the back pew and tried to imagine what it must have been like to be a real angel talking to the shepherds in the field. She wondered about Mary and Joseph and that tiny babe born in a manger. Was He cold? Did He care that He'd been born in such a stinky place?

After thinking awhile, Eleanor Jo's eyes grew heavy. She lay down on the back pew to rest her eyes for just a minute. Before she knew it, she was fast asleep.

Some time later, she awoke in a darkened church.

"Hello?" she called out.

No one responded.

A little shiver ran down her spine as she called out again. "Hello? Is anyone there?"

Still no response.

From outside the window, she could see a glimmer of light from nearby houses. She tiptoed to the door of the church and pushed it open, shivering against the cold.

"Mama? Papa?" She called out for her parents, but they did not answer.

She ran as fast as her legs could carry her to the road, crying out all the way. Finally, off in the distance, she heard the sound of people's voices singing Christmas carols. She ran in the direction of the sound until she came upon a crowd of friends and family members.

"Mama, Mama!" She pressed through the group of people until she reached her mother at last.

Mama turned around, surprised. "Yes, Eleanor Jo?"

"You left me at the church."

"What? You weren't with us?"

"No." Eleanor Jo began to whimper. "I woke up and it was dark inside. No one was there."

"Oh, darlin,'" Papa scooped her into his strong arms. "I'm so sorry that happened. We just got carried away with the Christmas festivities, I guess. How did you find us?"

Eleanor Jo leaned her head against Papa's shoulder. "I could hear the singing," she said. "Even from far away, the Christmas carols sounded like an angel choir."

"Well now, you see," Papa said, "the angels led you to us, and you're safe and sound. Praise the Lord for that!"

"Yes, praise the Lord!" Mama echoed.

Soon everyone returned to their singing. All but Eleanor Jo, who rested against Papa's shoulder and fell fast asleep once again.

*She sat in awe, watching the little
wooden elves as they moved back
and forth, back and forth, working in
Santa's Toy Shop. Some hammered,
others sawed. Still others filled Santa's
large bag with toys and goodies for
boys and girls. Eleanor Jo had never
seen anything like it before, and could
hardly believe she was seeing it now.*

THE TWO-DOLLAR
CHRISTMAS

*T*HE DAY BEFORE CHRISTMAS, PAPA sat the children down in the living room for what he called a "family talk." Eleanor Jo listened closely. She could hardly wait to hear what he had to say. She couldn't help but notice the wrinkles on his forehead as he spoke. He looked a little sad...but why?

He took off his hat and twisted it around in his hands a bit before speaking. "Mama and I have been thinking a lot about Christmas," he said finally.

Eleanor Jo's heart started racing. Yes indeed. He was going to tell them something very special. But why the sad look on his face?

"I'm afraid I need to start by telling you that this has been a very hard year." Papa spoke softly, and Eleanor Jo noticed his fingers gripping the brim of the hat a bit more tightly.

Mama reached over and squeezed his hand. "It's always hard, the first few years on a farm," she explained. "And things will be better next year, I'm sure of it."

"Still," Papa went on, "because money is so tight, we've had to make a decision about Christmas presents."

Martha Ann clapped her hands, and James shouted the word "present," but Eleanor Jo did not get excited. In fact, she had a feeling Papa's next few words were not going to be happy ones.

"This is what we've decided," Papa said. "Because we don't really have money to spend on gifts this year, Mama and I want to do something fun with you children, something we've never ever done before."

"N…no presents?" Martha Ann stammered.

Eleanor Jo put her finger to her lips, trying to shush her little sister. She could see the pain in Papa's eyes. No sense in hurting his feelings even more. And besides, she knew of one present already. She had seen the basket of fruit hidden away.

Eleanor Jo tried to put on her happiest face, the very happiest one she could manage. "What are we going to do, Papa?" she asked.

He offered up a warm smile. "Mama and I are going to take the money we have—two dollars—and use it to put gasoline in our car for a special road trip to Dallas."

"Dallas?" All of the children squealed at once.

"Oh, Papa, how wonderful!" Eleanor Jo bounced up and down. "I haven't been to the city since I was a little girl."

"That's right," Mama said with a grin. "You were just five the last time. And this time will be extra-special because we're going to see the windows at Neiman Marcus, a big, beautiful department store."

"Windows?" Martha Ann pouted. "Windows aren't any fun." She crossed her arms, and her lips curled down in disappointment.

"Oh, these are," Papa said with a wink. "In fact, you will think these are the prettiest windows in all the world, for they're *Christmas* windows."

"Christmas windows." Eleanor Jo repeated his words, wondering what in the world a Christmas window must look like.

"Hmph." Martha Ann still didn't look convinced.

"When will we go?" Eleanor Jo asked.

"That's the best news of all." Mama clapped her hands together in excitement. "We're leaving today. This very minute, in fact."

"W…what?" Eleanor Jo jumped up from her seat. "We're going today? To town?"

"Indeed," Papa answered. "So grab your coats, and let's get this show on the road."

Minutes later the family sat in the large black car, rolling down the highway. As they traveled along,

Eleanor Jo looked out of the window. Funny, now that the snow had melted, it didn't even feel like winter, let alone Christmas.

"Christmas." She whispered the word, and a pain filled her heart. If what Papa had said about the two dollars was true, there would be no gifts at all this year. None. A few tears came to her eyes, but she quickly brushed them away. No point in fretting over what she couldn't have. And besides, like Mama said, she already had the very best gift of all. Jesus was the greatest present ever.

As the family traveled along the road toward Dallas, they talked about the party at Mrs. Urschel's house, and Eleanor Jo told her parents about the gold faucet she had touched. Her mother just smiled and said, "That's lovely, Eleanor Jo," but Eleanor Jo wondered if Mama ever longed for such things. If so, she never said. No, Mama wasn't one to complain. Work hard, yes. Complain, no.

Papa dove into a conversation about the church play, and after that he started singing "Hark the Herald Angels Sing" at the top of his lungs. Just for fun, he rolled down the window of the car. "To let the praises out," he explained. Eleanor Jo giggled. Papa sure knew how to have a good time. Even in the middle of not-so-good times.

Before long, the family arrived in Dallas. Martha Ann squealed as they approached the center of town. "Look, look!" she cried. "Christmas! It's everywhere!"

And she was right. The streets were decorated every inch of the way. Colorful silver bells hung across the center of each intersection, and the light poles all along the way were covered in tinsel. Lights twinkled merrily in store windows, and for the first time Eleanor Jo understood what Papa had meant when he called them "Christmas windows."

"Is that Neiman Marcus?" she asked, pointing to a storefront.

"Oh no," Mama explained. "That's the five and dime. Neiman's is far larger than that. Just wait. You've never seen anything quite like it, I assure you."

Papa eased the car along through the holiday traffic. People walked along the sidewalks with Christmas packages in their hands. Their faces were lit with joy. Eleanor Jo took it all in with great excitement, but never stopped look, look, looking for the store windows her father had mentioned.

Finally they came into view. Eleanor Jo could scarcely believe her eyes. Through the large glass windows, colorful scenes glistened. Snowflakes and elves, Santas and reindeer. The sight was simply breathtaking.

"Oh, Papa!" Eleanor Jo marveled. "They're beautiful. Beautiful!"

"I knew you would like them." He flashed a broad smile.

She sat in awe, watching the little wooden elves as they moved back and forth, back and forth, working in Santa's Toy Shop. Some hammered, others sawed. Still others filled Santa's large bag with toys and goodies for boys and girls. Eleanor Jo had never seen anything like it before, and could hardly believe she was seeing it now.

"Slow down, Papa," she cried out. "I want to see it all."

"We'll be out of the car soon enough," Mama scolded. "Don't fret."

"Elves," James whispered with his nose glued to the car window. "I saw elves!" He looked up at Eleanor Jo. "Are they real?"

Eleanor Jo shook her head. "No, but they sure *look* real, don't they?"

"Uh-huh." He nodded, his eyes wide as saucers.

"Does Santa Claus shop at Neiman Marcus?" Martha Ann asked with a look of wonder on her face.

Papa let out a belly laugh. "I doubt that he could afford to."

Mama joined in, and before you knew it, they were all laughing. Papa parked the car in a large parking lot, and the children followed him along the sidewalk at the front of the store. All along the way, they paused to look in the windows. Eleanor Jo could scarcely breathe. The whole thing was just too…lovely.

"Papa, look at the nutcracker," she whispered. She stared in silence at the window scene filled with brightly colored nutcrackers and ballerinas. In truth, she had never witnessed anything as marvelous.

"Mama," Martha Ann shouted, "Look at the ballerina! She's dancing."

Sure enough, the little wooden ballerina with the pink painted skirt moved about in circles. Every now and again her leg lifted, lifted, lifted into the air, and she twirled with grace. Next to her, a giant nutcracker wagged his head back and forth, back and forth.

"How do they do that?" Martha Ann whispered.

"Is it magic?" Eleanor Jo echoed.

Papa shook his head. "Might look like magic, but it's not. They run on tracks. See there," he said as he pointed.

"Wow!" All of the children said at the same time.

Eleanor Jo watched in rapture as they moved from window to window. She whispered a little prayer, thanking the Lord for such a wonderful Christmas present.

"Papa..." she whispered the word, looking up at her father.

"What, pumpkin?"

She wiggled her finger, and he leaned down to hear her next words. "This is the very best Christmas ever," she said.

Papa scooped her up into his arms and gave her a kiss on the forehead. "I knew you would like it," he whispered back. "I just knew it."

They stood there for a while before going into the store. Mama commented on the glitter in the nutcracker's vest, and Martha Ann licked her lips at the sight of the colorful lollipops lining the inside edges of the window. James bounced up and down, tickled at the notion that Christmas could be found in a window.

And Eleanor Jo whispered a silent prayer, one that only the Lord heard. She thanked Him, from the bottom of her heart, for this amazing two-dollar Christmas.

As she entered the kitchen, Eleanor Jo and the others stopped in amazement. The kitchen table was loaded with goodies—cakes, pies, breads, and lots of vegetables. And in the very middle of the table, was a turkey, ready for baking.

A CHRISTMAS MIRACLE

*A*FTER ELEANOR JO AND HER FAMILY looked at the Christmas windows, they ventured inside Neiman Marcus. The large department store was beautifully decorated with Christmas frills. People milled about with packages in their arms. Mothers and fathers guided their children along through the crowd. And what a crowd! Eleanor Jo wasn't sure when she'd ever seen more people in all of her life.

Papa snatched James up into his arms, and Martha Ann clutched Mama's hand. Eleanor Jo found it difficult to remember to keep up with her parents. How could she, with so many things to look at? She kept pausing to look at the beautiful things along the way.

Mama's hand reached down to grab hers. "Hold tightly to my hand, honey," she said.

They made their way through the large store to the toy department, where Martha Ann at once began to squeal. "Oh, Papa! Look at all the dolls. And the marionettes! Oh, Mama, aren't they beautiful!"

Eleanor Jo started to join in but quickly changed her mind. She knew that her parents could not afford to buy such things. To go on and on about them would surely hurt their feelings.

After a lengthy walk through the store, Papa announced it was time to go home.

"We have a long drive ahead of us," he said. "And it will be dark soon, so we'd better get a move on."

Eleanor Jo was sorry to see her visit to town come to an end, but she was growing a little tired and oh so hungry. Once inside the car, Mama fed everyone sandwiches she had brought from home. Afterward, as Papa drove, Eleanor Jo closed her eyes and tried to sleep.

Just as her eyelids fluttered closed, the image of the ballerina danced before her eyes. How beautiful to be able to dance like that. And how lovely the nutcrackers were. The whole day had been simply wonderful. Almost wonderful enough to take her mind off of the empty spot under the tree at home.

After a while, sleep took over, and Eleanor Jo dreamed of Christmas windows. In her dream, she could reach through the glass and grab hold of one of the lollipops, which she handed to her little sister. Martha Ann's face lit up with glee.

Eleanor Jo slept soundly until her mother's voice awakened her.

"What in the world?" Mama sounded afraid as she spoke the words.

Eleanor Jo sat up in the car and rubbed her eyes, realizing they had arrived home. "What's wrong, Mama?" she asked.

"Someone's been in our house," Papa said, as he pulled the car into the long, narrow driveway. "They've left the light on in the living room. Front porch too."

"Oh no," Mama whispered. "I hope they haven't stolen anything."

Everyone sat in stillness for a moment, till James hollered out, "I'm sleepy, Mama."

"I know, darling."

Eleanor Jo shushed her little brother the best she could while Papa got out of the car. "I want all of you to wait here," he said with a look of concern on his face.

Everyone waited as he went toward the house. Eleanor Jo held her breath and prayed silently. "Lord, please take care of Papa. Don't let anything happen to him."

Moments later he appeared at the car, with a look of amazement on his face. "Come with me!" His eyes were flooded with tears.

"What is it, honey?" Mama asked, putting her hand to her heart. "What's happened?"

"Come and see."

Everyone tumbled from the car, and Papa led the way to the house. As he swung open the living room door, Martha Ann let out a squeal, "Oh, Papa! Christmas!"

Eleanor Jo looked around the room in shock and surprise. The area underneath the tree was filled with presents, beautifully wrapped. "Oh, Mama," she whispered. "How did you do this?"

"I didn't," Mama whispered back. "I haven't got a clue what has happened here." She erupted in tears, and Papa's eyes spilled over as well.

For a few seconds, nobody said a thing. Finally Martha Ann ran to the tree and started looking through the presents. "I see one with my name on it. May I open it?"

"Tomorrow morning, darling." Mama patted her on the head. "We must wait till Christmas morning."

Martha Ann pouted once again.

After looking over the gifts, Mama headed to the kitchen. Eleanor Jo raced to join her when Mama let out a cry.

"Oh, my!" Mama said. "It's not possible."

As she entered the kitchen, Eleanor Jo and the others stopped in amazement. The kitchen table was loaded with goodies—cakes, pies, breads, and lots of vegetables. And in the very middle of the table, was a turkey, ready for baking.

"Thank You, Jesus." Mama sat in a kitchen chair and leaned her head down on the table in prayer. "You've been too good to us. Too good."

"Look at the cookies, Mama!" Martha Ann pointed to a tray of Snickerdoodles. "Yummy! Can I have one?"

"You can!" Papa reached to grab a handful of cookies and passed them around, not even waiting to see the look on Mama's face. Would she scold?

No, Mama wasn't mad. She lifted her tear-stained face and extended her hand, reaching for a cookie. "I want one too," she whispered. "Possibly two."

Papa smiled as he handed her two of the cinnamon and sugar-coated delights. Everyone nibbled on their cookies for a minute or two in quiet. Then Papa began to laugh, his rich laughter filling the kitchen. Before you knew it, Mama was laughing too. Then Eleanor Jo, and then the little ones.

Round and round, the laughter went. The whole family stayed in the kitchen until the giggling stopped. Then Papa led them into the living room once again. As he reached the tree, he burst into song. The sound of "O Come All Ye Faithful" filled the air. Soon everyone was singing.

O come, all ye faithful, joyful and triumphant,
O come ye, O come ye to Bethlehem.
Come and behold Him, born the King of angels.

O come, let us adore Him, O come, let us adore Him,
O come, let us adore Him, Christ, the Lord.

As Eleanor Jo opened her eyes, a sense of wonder set in. She looked across the room at her family as they sang praises to the Lord. She thought back to the day she and Martha Ann had sung their praises in the snow and smiled. Seemed like the past few days had been filled with praises.

And what a lot they had to be thankful for! The past week had brought with it many miracles—the fluffy white snow, the party at Mrs. Urschel's house, the Christmas play, the beautiful Christmas windows at Neiman Marcus, and now the presents and Christmas foods. Her heart could hardly contain it all. She closed her eyes once again, trying not to cry as the music rang out.

O come, let us adore Him, O come, let us adore Him,
O come, let us adore Him, Christ, the Lord.

Eleanor Jo closed her eyes as they sang the chorus over and over again. A sense of joy and peace filled her heart—not because there were now presents under the tree, but because the love of Jesus completely filled her up, from head to toe.

Martha Ann woke up Eleanor Jo with a shout. "Get up, get up! It's Christmas morning!" she hollered.

A JOYOUS CHRISTMAS

ARTHA ANN WOKE UP ELEANOR JO with a shout. "Get up, get up! It's Christmas morning!" she hollered.

Eleanor Jo rubbed her eyes and looked across the dark room at the window. "It's not even light out yet. Mama and Papa are probably still asleep."

"But it's Christmas." Martha Ann pulled at her arm. "And we have presents. Lots of presents."

"Fine, fine." Eleanor Jo shivered as she scrambled from the bed. After putting on her robe, she followed Martha Ann into the kitchen, where she found Mama cooking pancakes.

"Merry Christmas, daughters!" Mama said.

"Merry Christmas, Mama!" Eleanor Jo threw her arms around her mother's waist. "Where's Papa?"

"Gone out to fetch the ham from the smokehouse," Mama explained. "He will be back shortly."

"Can we open presents when he gets back?" Martha Ann asked.

"Presents, presents!" James echoed, appearing in the kitchen doorway.

Mama patted him on the head. "You haven't even wiped the sleep from your eyes," she said with a smile.

He rubbed at his eyes, and then looked up with a crooked grin. "Now presents?"

"Not till after breakfast," Mama said.

Papa appeared at the door in his work clothes with the ham in hand. "Merry Christmas, family!" He held it up for all to see.

"Merry Christmas, Papa!" they all answered.

He handed Mama the ham, which she quickly prepared and placed in the oven alongside the turkey. Then Papa joined them at the table, and they ate some of Mama's fluffy pancakes and sausage. Eleanor Jo could hardly think about food, however. Her mind was on the presents in the other room.

Finally the time came. They all made their way into the living room where the beautiful tree awaited.

"How shall we do this?" Mama asked.

Papa reached for one of the gifts and handed it to Mama. "One at a time," he suggested.

One by one, the gifts were opened. Mama received a beautiful hand-crocheted shawl. Her eyes misted over as she held it up. "What a pretty shade of blue," she said.

James opened a package with a wooden pull-toy inside in the shape of a colorful duck. "Ooo!" He jumped up and began to pull the duck around the room. It made a funny quacking sound, and everyone laughed.

Next, Martha Ann opened up a package with her name on it. Inside was a box of tiny china dishes, just the right size for a tea party. "Oh, Mama," she cried. "They're so pretty! I can't wait to invite my friends over for a party!"

Finally it was Eleanor Jo's turn. She reached to open a package with her name on it, and found the prettiest doll she had ever seen. It had a fancy ivory-colored dress and a porcelain face. She clutched the doll in her arms and rocked it back and forth. "I've never had anything so beautiful," she whispered. "I'm going to name her Shirley after Shirley Temple."

Papa opened up a package with a leather belt inside. "Well, if that doesn't beat all," he said. "And I've been needing a new belt!"

They went around the circle again, each opening another present. This time Mama got a bonnet. Martha Ann got a Raggedy Ann doll, which she promptly pretended to feed a cup of tea. James opened a toy truck, and Eleanor Jo unwrapped a beautiful hat with matching gloves. Papa's last gift turned out to be a pocketknife. Everyone had a grand time, laughing and talking until the room grew quite loud.

Still, one present remained under the tree. There was no name on this one. "Must be for the family," Papa said.

All of the children worked together to unwrap it.

"Oh, Mama!" Eleanor Jo stood back in awe as she looked at the nativity scene. "It's the stable."

"And the animals!" Martha Ann reached down to pick up a tiny wooden lamb.

"Donkey! Road-ee!" James squealed as he picked up a small carved donkey.

"This donkey is a little more handsome than Road-ee," Mama said as she reached to touch the top of the stable. "But who in the world could have done this for us?" She looked up at Papa, who gave a shrug.

"Whoever it is—and I think it must've been a whole lot of folks—must love our family a lot."

Eleanor Jo surely felt loved as she looked around the room—not just because of the presents, but because someone had taken the time to make sure they had the best Christmas ever. Mrs. Urschel, perhaps? Pastor Weathers and his family?

Maybe they would never know.

After opening the presents, Mama presented the basket of fruit. Eleanor Jo put on her most surprised face. Then, for the next couple of hours, the children played with their toys while Mama fixed Christmas dinner. Eleanor Jo finally set her doll down long enough to offer to help in the kitchen.

"You can mash the potatoes," Mama said as she handed her the large bowl of potatoes and the masher.

Eleanor Jo poured in a bit of cream and added a spoonful of butter to the potatoes before mashing them. Then she pounded away, doing all she could to make the potatoes as light and fluffy as Mama's. In the meantime, her mother kept an eye on the turkey and ham in the oven to make sure she didn't overcook them. Martha Ann set the table, and even James helped by folding the napkins.

Finally the moment came. Mama called everyone to the table. Papa appeared in the doorway with a broad smile on his face.

"Looks good enough to eat!" he teased.

"Well, it had better!" Mama pulled her homemade hot rolls out of the oven. "I've worked all morning."

As they sat at the table, Eleanor Jo looked over the food and licked her lips. Sweet potatoes, green beans, mashed potatoes, gravy, turkey, dressing, cranberries, ham…she could hardly wait.

"Let's pray." Papa stretched out his arms, and they all joined hands to pray together. He thanked the Lord for the food set before them. He also thanked Him for the amazing gifts they had been given.

Before you knew it, everyone was eating and talking, all at once. Eleanor Jo put big spoonfuls of mashed potatoes into her mouth and swallowed them down.

"You did a great job mashing these, darling," her mother said with a smile.

Eleanor Jo beamed with delight. Nothing felt better than making Mama proud.

"I told you," Papa said with a wink, "one of these days you're going to grow up and have a family of your own to cook for. You'll make the best mashed potatoes in town, because you've learned from the very best cook in all the world!"

Everyone giggled, and Mama's cheeks turned pink. But right now Eleanor Jo couldn't even imagine what it must feel like to be grown up. Not on a day like today, when being a little girl was so much fun. No, she would much rather play with dolls and help her mother mash potatoes than think about grown-up things—at least for now.

Mama nodded as tears filled her eyes. "Mine too. I've always loved this season. And it doesn't have anything to do with presents or parties or even Christmas windows. It's because every year at Christmas, I'm reminded of what God did for us."

THE REASON
FOR THE SEASON

FTER DINNER, PAPA BUILT A ROARING
fire in the fireplace, and the family
settled down in the living room to
visit. Mama poured a steaming cup of coffee for Papa,
and he leaned back in his chair, quiet and content. Mama
sat in the rocker with James in her lap. She rocked him
back and forth until his eyes grew heavy.

Martha Ann stretched out in the middle of the rug to
play with her doll, and Eleanor Jo sat beside her, joining
in the fun. For a few minutes, no one said anything.

Finally Mama broke the silence. She ran her fingers
through James's hair as she spoke. "You know," she said,
"I do believe this Christmas has turned out to be the very
best one yet."

Everyone nodded in unison.

"If you think about it, we've had quite a week," she
said. "First the snow."

"Then the snow angels!" Martha Ann said with a little giggle.

"Cutting down the tree together," Papa added.

"And decorating the house," Mama reminded them.

"Baking cookies for the party!" Eleanor Jo chimed in.

"Seeing the inside of Mrs. Urschel's beautiful home," Mama said with a dreamy look in her eye.

"Eating candy canes!" Martha Ann squealed.

"Singing the solo at church," Eleanor Jo said softly.

"Driving to town to see the Christmas windows," Papa reminded them.

"Finding presents under the tree when we got home." Eleanor Jo spoke the words, still remembering what it felt like to see those gifts under their Christmas tree.

"And the food!" Mama shook her head, as if she still couldn't quite believe it. "Finding all of that food in our kitchen!"

"We are a blessed family." Papa spoke quietly, and then stood to tend to the fire in the fireplace. "Blessed indeed."

As everyone grew quiet, Eleanor Jo thought about all of the many gifts of the past week. So much had happened, but nothing compared to one thing. "My favorite part," she said, "was praising God in the snow."

"Praising God in the snow?" Mama asked.

Eleanor Jo and Martha Ann both nodded at the same time, and then stretched out on the floor to show Mama and Papa how they had called out, "Glory to God in the highest" while making snow angels.

Papa's face broke into a broad smile, and he came to lift Eleanor Jo into his arms. "You girls are the closest things to real angels," he said. "And I'm so proud of you. Both of you. To think…singing praises to God was your favorite part of the week."

He put her back down, and sat once again in his chair, shaking his head.

"Have I said something to upset you, Papa?" Eleanor Jo asked as she climbed into his lap.

He leaned his whiskery chin against her head and whispered, "No, darlin'. I'm not sad. I always get a little misty-eyed around Christmastime. It's my favorite time of the year."

Mama nodded as tears filled her eyes. "Mine too. I've always loved this season. And it doesn't have anything to do with presents or parties or even Christmas windows. It's because every year at Christmas, I'm reminded of what God did for us."

Eleanor Jo leaned her head against Papa's shoulder and listened as he spoke. "God loves us all so much," he said. "But He knew that we needed a Savior. And to think…He was willing to send His Son to earth to be born as a baby in a manger."

Eleanor Jo took her baby doll and rocked it in her arms. Perhaps this was what Mary felt like when she rocked baby Jesus back and forth in her arms that Christmas morning so long ago.

"The best part of the Christmas story doesn't take place on Christmas, though," Papa added.

"It doesn't?" Martha Ann looked confused.

"No." Papa shook his head. "See, the best part of the Christmas story happened many, many years later, when Jesus was all grown up. In fact, He was about the same age I am now."

Eleanor Jo listened closely as Papa went on to tell them about Jesus growing into a man. He told how Jesus lived a sinless life, never hurting anyone or doing anything wrong. And then Papa began to tell a part of the story that was very, very sad.

"Some people didn't believe that Jesus was the Son of God at all. They didn't know that He was a gift, a present. In the end, they…" Papa's voice trailed off and his eyes filled with tears.

"What did they do, Papa?" Eleanor Jo asked. "What did they do to Jesus?"

His voice was soft as he answered. "They crucified Him on a cross."

"Crucified?" Martha Ann echoed. "What does that mean?"

Eleanor Jo was pretty sure she knew, but didn't say. Her heart *thump-thumped* as she waited for Papa's answer.

"He died that day." Mama whispered the words, and tears dripped from her lashes.

"But why?" Now Eleanor Jo had tears in her eyes too. "Why would they do that to Him if He never hurt anyone?"

"They simply didn't understand that Jesus was the Savior of the world," Papa said sadly. Then suddenly his sad face changed to a happy one. "But the truth is, no one took His life. He gave it."

"Gave it?" Eleanor Jo asked. "What do you mean?"

"He chose to go to the cross for our sins."

"For my sins?" Martha Ann asked.

"And mine too?" Eleanor Jo echoed.

Papa nodded. "And mine. And Mama's. And James's too. He did it for all of the people in the world—because He loves us. When Jesus died on the cross, He took all of the bad things I ever did—and all of the bad things you ever did—and He wiped them away like they never happened, like we never did anything wrong at all."

"He did that for me?" Eleanor Jo could hardly believe it. "Why did Jesus have to die for me?"

"You'll find the answer to that question in the Bible," Papa said. "John 3:16 says, 'For God so loved the world, that he gave his only begotten Son, that whosoever believeth in him should not perish, but have everlasting life.' See, God gave us the best gift of all—far greater than any you could find under a tree. He gave us the gift of salvation."

"Salvation." Martha Ann said the word slowly. "What does it mean?"

"It means He makes us white as snow."

"White as snow?" Eleanor Jo whispered the words. "Snow is *very* white."

"Yes, and your heart can be just as white." Papa's eyes lit up as he went on. "Eleanor Jo, you're a big girl, and I can't think of a better time than Christmas to ask Jesus to live in your heart, to make you as white as that snow you and your little sister played in the other day. Would you like to do that?"

"Oh, yes, Papa!" Eleanor Jo could hardly keep the tears from falling as she answered. Would Jesus really make her heart white as snow?

"Me too, Papa!" Martha Ann echoed.

Papa asked the girls to pray a prayer with him. He started it, and they repeated after him. "Lord Jesus," he prayed, "please forgive me of all my sins and come and live in my heart this Christmas day. I accept You as my Savior, and I invite You to be the Lord of my life. Thank You for dying on the cross for me and for being the very best Christmas present of all!"

Eleanor Jo said all of the words along with Papa and meant every one. When she finished praying, she opened her eyes and looked up at her father. Tears streamed down his face.

"Papa!" she said. "I did it!"

"You did." He grinned. "And would you like to know what the angels—the *real* ones, up in heaven—are doing right now?"

"What?"

"They're celebrating!" Papa laughed out loud. "They're celebrating because you and Martha Ann have received the greatest gift of all!"

Eleanor Jo leaned back against Papa's chest and thought about what he had said. Right now—this very minute—the angels are celebrating. Just like they had the night Jesus was born. But tonight they celebrated because she and Martha Ann had accepted the free gift of salvation.

Suddenly Eleanor Jo felt like celebrating too. She sprang up from the chair and grabbed her sister's hands. Together they danced around the room, shouting, "Glory to God in the highest! Glory to God in the highest!"

James awoke from his nap and rubbed his eyes. Then he jumped from Mama's lap and linked arms with his sisters. They all turned in circles, celebrating the joyous news of Christmas.

—⟫●⟪—

"This has been the most perfect Christmas ever," Eleanor Jo sighed. "As long as I live, I don't think I will ever have a better one."

—⟫●⟪—

THE BEST
CHRISTMAS EVER

*L*ATER THAT EVENING, ELEANOR JO TOOK A bath in the metal washtub and then towel-dried her long hair. Mama ran a brush through it and began to French braid it. All the while, they sang Christmas carols together. The sound of their voices rang out across the house. From the other room, Eleanor Jo could hear Papa's deep voice chiming in. She let out a little giggle. Truthfully, she didn't know when she had ever had more fun.

"Oh, Mama," she said, finally. "This has been the best day ever. Does it have to end?"

"I don't want it to," Martha Ann said with a pout.

Mama shook her head as she explained. "It doesn't have to end. Not really."

"It doesn't?" they both echoed.

"No." Their mother's eyes sparkled as she spoke. "Christmas day is almost over, but that doesn't mean we stop celebrating. The celebration can go on and on."

"We can have Christmas all year round?" Eleanor Jo asked, as she slipped on her nightgown.

"We can." Mama flashed a warm smile. "See, when Jesus lives in your heart, it's Christmas every day of the year!"

"Christmas every day!" Martha Ann jumped up and down on the bed as she spoke. "How fun!"

"Stop that jumping on the bed, Martha Ann," Mama scolded.

Eleanor Jo's little sister sat down right away but couldn't seem to stop giggling. "If it's Christmas every day, can we have a candy cane every day?" she asked.

Mama shook her head and sighed. "Absolutely not. All of that sugar wouldn't be good for your teeth!"

"Who cares about teeth, anyway?" Martha Ann asked.

They laughed for so long that Papa finally hollered from outside the door. "What in the world is going on in there? Are you girls having a party?"

"Yes," Mama answered. "We're celebrating!"

"Don't have too much fun without me," Papa said.

"We won't!" they all answered.

Eleanor Jo thought about her Mama's words as she helped braid Martha Ann's hair. Now that Jesus lived in her heart, she could spend every day celebrating.

Just before climbing under the quilt with her little sister, Eleanor Jo decided one more adventure was in order. "May I go into the living room for a minute?" she asked.

"This late?" Mama gave her a funny look. "What for?"

Eleanor Jo shrugged. "There's something I want to do."

"Don't be too long." Mama gave her a wink.

With her baby doll tucked underneath her arm, Eleanor Jo tiptoed down the hallway for another teensy-tiny peek at the Christmas tree. The space under the tree was empty now, but her heart surely didn't feel empty. In fact, she didn't know when she had ever felt better.

She walked over to the manger scene and stared down at the wood-carved baby Jesus inside. She thought about the story Papa had told—how Jesus grew into a man and died on a cross. "For me," she whispered. "For me."

Just for fun, Eleanor Jo replaced the baby in the manger with her doll. Shirley barely fit into the little manger, but Eleanor Jo didn't mind.

As she stared down at the baby, she hummed a little lullaby. She closed her eyes, and tried to imagine what it must have been like on the night the shepherds came to the stable to see baby Jesus for the first time. Did He look like her little doll, safely tucked away in the manger? Did the shepherds really know that the baby they were looking at was the Savior of the world?

"Still up, darling?" Papa appeared in the doorway.

Eleanor Jo nodded. "Just for a minute." She gave him a smile and then pointed to the tree. "Papa, who do you think did all of this for us? Mrs. Urschel?"

He shrugged. "I really don't know, but whoever went to the trouble to give us such a wonderful Christmas deserves an extra-special blessing this year, that's for sure."

At that moment, something at the window caught Eleanor Jo's attention. "Oh, Papa!" She ran toward the window with a squeal.

"What is it, honey?"

"Look!" She whispered the word as she pointed at the white flakes tumbling down from the sky. "I don't believe it. It's snowing again!"

"Well, I'll be…" He joined her at the window, and together they stared in silence at the white flurries as they hit the ground.

"This has been the most perfect Christmas ever," Eleanor Jo sighed. "As long as I live, I don't think I will ever have a better one."

"Oh, darlin'…" He reached over to give her a kiss on the cheek, "I wouldn't be so sure of that. I dare say there will be many, many more wonderful Christmases in the years ahead for you."

"Do you think so?" She turned to face him.

"Oh yes," Papa said. He reached to brush a loose hair from her eyes. "When you are quite grown-up, you will look back on this Christmas with fond memories. But remember, little one—your best days are ahead."

"My best days are ahead." Eleanor Jo whispered the words, and leaned her head against Papa's arm.

Funny, no matter how hard she tried, she couldn't imagine anything better than today. This had truly been the best Christmas ever.

"One day," Grand Doll said, "you will tell your children the Christmas story, and they will understand that God sent His Son into the world for them."

HOLLY'S CHRISTMAS LESSON

OLLY LISTENED TO HER GRAND-
mother's story with great excitement.
"Oh, Grand Doll!" she said. "That
story was about you! You're little Eleanor Jo."

"That's right," Grand Doll said, as she clasped her
hands together in glee. "I was once a little girl just like
you. I'll bet that's pretty hard to imagine."

"Not at all!" Holly said. In fact, she had no trouble
imagining her grandmother as little Eleanor Jo, making
snow angels with her younger sister. "I loved your
Christmas story."

"I'm so glad." Grand Doll looked across the breakfast
table at her grandchildren. "Do you remember that I told
you all in the beginning about a gift that keeps on giving
and giving?"

"Yes ma'am." Holly nodded. "You were talking about
Jesus."

"That's right. You heard what I said about asking Jesus to come and live in my heart. My papa led me in that prayer. And I led my children in the very same prayer many years later. And my children—your father, in fact—led you in that prayer just one year ago."

"Yes." Holly smiled. She remembered the day she had prayed with her father. What a wonderful day that had been!

"One day," Grand Doll said, "you will tell your children the Christmas story, and they will understand that God sent His Son into the world for them."

Holly nodded. "May I ask you a question?"

"Of course!" Grand Doll's eyes lit up. "You know I love your questions!"

"Did you ever find out who left all of the presents under your tree?"

"And who left all the food?" Chelsea added.

"You know…" Grand Doll's eyes filled with tears, "we never did find out. Papa asked several of our friends, and so did Mama, but no one ever told us. I dare say, we had our very own Christmas angel that year."

Everyone grew silent for a moment as they thought about Grand Doll's amazing story. "The presents under the tree weren't the best gift that year," she reminded them. "But they were a lot of fun. And they taught me that God uses His people to love one another—at

Christmastime and all year round. I try to share that love with people every chance I get."

"Is that why you took presents to the church last night?" Holly asked.

Grand Doll nodded. "Yes. Every Christmas I choose one family to bless. This year I bought a porcelain doll for one of the little girls in our church. Her father is out of work, and her mother is very sick."

"I want to bless others," Holly said.

"Me too," Chelsea echoed.

Grand Doll's face lit with excitement. "You can! Next year we will all go shopping together. We'll have a grand time blessing others. But in the meantime, I want you children to know what a blessing you are to me and to Poppie."

"That's right." Poppie nodded.

"Thank you, Grand Doll." Holly gave a little giggle. "I love being a blessing."

Her grandmother's face grew quite serious. "You've been a blessing all along. A miracle blessing, I should add."

All of the adults in the room nodded, but Holly was confused.

"Miracle blessing?" she asked. "What do you mean?"

Grand Doll's eyes grew large as she said, "Don't you know the story, honey? About how we almost lost our little Christmas Holly before she was born?"

Holly listened closely. She had never heard this story.

"I received a phone call on the day you were supposed to be born," Grand Doll explained. "Something was wrong. The doctor was afraid you wouldn't make it."

Holly looked up at her mother who nodded with a sad look on her face.

"It was a scary time," Mama added.

"Really? Wow." Holly thought about that for a moment. She couldn't even imagine how different things would be if she hadn't been born.

"We all prayed," Poppie said. "All of us."

"And you came into the world, safe and sound!" Grand Doll chuckled. "An honest-to-goodness Christmas miracle, with a Christmas-y name too!"

Holly shook her head, amazed at the story. "I didn't know that," she whispered.

"It's true!" Right away, Grand Doll began to sing the Sans Day Carol. Before long, everyone in the room joined in:

And Mary bore Jesus our Saviour for to be,
And the first tree in the greenwood, it was
the holly.
Holly! Holly!
And the first tree in the greenwood, it was
the holly!

As they finished singing, Grand Doll clapped her hands to get everyone's attention. "Now, who wants some hot chocolate and tea cakes?" she asked.

"Me, me!" they all shouted.

With great excitement, they all started chattering. All but Holly Marie. She went into the living room and gazed at the baby in the manger. She reached down to touch it, thinking about Grand Doll's story. She wondered if her grandmother still thought a lot about that Christmas, all those years ago. Was it truly the best one ever or were her best days ahead? Perhaps she would ask her later.

"Are you coming, Holly Marie?" Grand Doll's voice rang out from the kitchen.

"I'm coming!" she answered.

And with a smile on her face, she skipped off to the kitchen to join the others.

How does your family celebrate Christmas?

_____

_____

_____

_____

_____

_____

_____

_____

_____

_____

How did your parents celebrate Christmas when they were children? (If you don't know, ask them.)

How did your grandparents celebrate Christmas when they were children?

What is your favorite Christmas tradition?

_____

_____

_____

_____

_____

_____

_____

_____

_____

_____

_____

_____

What is the best Christmas present you ever received?

_____

_____

_____

_____

_____

_____

_____

_____

_____

_____

_____

_____

_____

What is the best Christmas present you ever gave someone else?

_____

_____

_____

_____

_____

_____

_____

_____

_____

_____

_____

_____

_____

What are some things that you and your family can do for friends or families who are less fortunate during the Christmas season?

_____

_____

_____

_____

_____

_____

_____

_____

_____

_____

_____

_____

Do you understand what people mean when they say, "Jesus is the reason for the season?" Explain.

_____

_____

_____

_____

_____

_____

_____

_____

_____

_____

_____

Write about your best Christmas ever.

What are some of your favorite things about Christmas (such as decorating the house, trimming the tree, shopping, baking, presents, etc.)?

_____

_____

_____

_____

_____

_____

_____

_____

_____

_____

_____

_____

What is a tradition that you can start with your family next Christmas?

Fun Facts
and More

DID YOU KNOW THESE FUN CHRISTMAS FACTS FROM AMERICAN HISTORY?

§ People traditionally give gifts at Christmastime because the Wise Men brought gifts to young Jesus.

§ The Puritans banned the observation of Christmas. Those who were caught celebrating the holiday had to pay a fine.

§ In 1836, Alabama was the first state to legally celebrate Christmas.

§ Christmas trees were first sold in New York in 1851. That same year, a minister in Cleveland almost lost his job because he allowed a Christmas tree in his church.

§ During the Civil War, the North and South were divided over the celebration of Christmas.

§ In 1897, a newspaper editor responded to a letter from a little girl named Virginia, who had written to ask if there was a Santa Claus. His response: "Yes, Virginia, there is a Santa Claus" became quite famous.

§ In 1939, a gentleman from the Montgomery Ward Company created a funny little poem about Rudolph, one of Santa's reindeer, which became very popular. To this day, "Rudolph, the Red-Nosed Reindeer" is a favorite at Christmastime.

§ Christmas cards became popular in the nineteenth century.

§ Throughout the years, American Christmas trees have been decorated with a variety of objects, including homemade ornaments, lighted candles, cookies, apples, popcorn, and even nuts.

§ Most Christian churches these days hold an annual Christmas pageant to remind people of the real reason for the season.

The Best Gift

HAVE YOU EVER ASKED JESUS—THE BEST gift of all—to come and live inside your heart? Would you like to do that now? If so, pray the following prayer and mean it in your heart:

Dear Lord,

I come to You in the name of Jesus. I am a sinner. I've messed up a lot. I'm really sorry for all of my sins. Please forgive me. Make me white as snow. I believe that Your Son, Jesus, came to earth and lived a sinless life. I believe He died on the cross for me and shed His blood for my sins. I believe He rose from the dead. I choose right now to make Jesus Christ the Lord of my life. I accept Him as my Lord and Savior. I believe I am now His child! Thank You, Jesus, for what You did for me. Amen.

The Christmas Story

LUKE 2:1-20

AND IT CAME TO PASS IN THOSE DAYS, that there went out a decree from Caesar Augustus, that all the world should be taxed. (And this taxing was first made when Cyrenius was governor of Syria.) And all went to be taxed, every one into his own city.

And Joseph also went up from Galilee, out of the city of Nazareth, into Judaea, unto the city of David, which is called Bethlehem; (because he was of the house and lineage of David:) to be taxed with Mary his espoused wife, being great with child. And so it was, that, while they were there, the days were accomplished that she should be delivered. And she brought forth her firstborn son, and wrapped him in swaddling clothes, and laid him in a manger; because there was no room for them in the inn.

And there were in the same country shepherds abiding in the field, keeping watch over their flock by night. And, lo, the angel of the Lord came upon them, and the glory of the Lord shone round about them: and they were sore afraid. And the angel said unto them, Fear not: for, behold, I bring you good tidings of great joy, which shall be to all people.

For unto you is born this day in the city of David a Saviour, which is Christ the Lord.

And this shall be a sign unto you; Ye shall find the babe wrapped in swaddling clothes, lying in a manger. And suddenly there was with the angel a multitude of the heavenly host praising God, and saying, Glory to God in the highest, and on earth peace, good will toward men.

And it came to pass, as the angels were gone away from them into heaven, the shepherds said one to another, Let us now go even unto Bethlehem, and see this thing which is come to pass, which the Lord hath made known unto us. And they came with haste, and found Mary, and Joseph, and the babe lying in a manger.

And when they had seen it, they made known abroad the saying which was told them concerning this child. And all they that heard it wondered at those things which were told them by the shepherds. But Mary kept all these things, and pondered them in her heart.

And the shepherds returned, glorifying and praising God for all the things that they had heard and seen, as it was told unto them.

Sans Day
Carol

Now the holly bears a berry as white as the milk,
And Mary bore Jesus, all wrapped up in silk:

And Mary bore Jesus our Savior for to be,
And the first tree in the greenwood, it was the holly.
Holly! Holly!
And the first tree in the greenwood, it was the holly!

Now the holly bears a berry as green as the grass,
And Mary bore Jesus, who died on the cross:

And Mary bore Jesus our Savior for to be,
And the first tree in the greenwood, it was the holly.
Holly! Holly!
And the first tree in the greenwood, it was the holly!

Now the holly bears a berry as black as the coal,
And Mary bore Jesus, who died for us all:

And Mary bore Jesus our Savior for to be,
And the first tree in the greenwood, it was the holly.

Holly! Holly!
And the first tree in the greenwood, it was the holly!

Now the holly bears a berry, as blood is it red,
Then trust we our Savior, who rose from the dead:

And Mary bore Jesus our Savior for to be,
And the first tree in the greenwood, it was the holly.
Holly! Holly!
And the first tree in the greenwood, it was the holly!

The "Sans Day Carol" is a Christmas carol about the nativity of Jesus. It is from Gwennap, Cornwall, a county of England. The song is named for St. Day, an English saint.

The Eleanor Series

ELEANOR CLARK CONCEIVED THE IDEA for *The Eleanor Series* while researching her family's rich American history. Motivated by her family lineage, which had been traced back to the early 17th century, a God-ordained idea emerged: the legacy left by her ancestors provided the perfect tool to reach today's children with the timeless truths of patriotism, godly character, and miracles of faith. Through her own family's stories, she instills in children a love of God and country, along with a passion for history. With that in mind, she set out to craft this collection of novels for the youth of today. Each story in *The Eleanor Series* focuses on a particular character trait, and is laced with the pioneering spirit of one of Eleanor's true-to-life family members. These captivating stories span generations, are historically accurate, and highlight the nation's Christian heritage of faith. Twenty-first century readers—both children and parents—are sure to relate to these amazing character-building stories of young American's while learning Christian values and American history.

Look for all of these books in the Eleanor Series:

Christmas Book—*Eleanor Jo: A Christmas to Remember*
ISBN-10: 0-9753036-6-X
ISBN-13: 978-0-9753036-6-5

Available in 2007

Book One—*Mary Elizabeth: Welcome to America*
ISBN-10: 0-9753036-7-8
ISBN-13: 978-0-9753036-7-2

Book Two—*Victoria Grace: Courageous Patriot*
ISBN-10: 0-9753036-8-6
ISBN-13: 978-0-9753036-8-9

Book Three—*Katie Sue: Heading West*
ISBN-10: 0-9788726-0-6
ISBN-13: 978-0-9788726-0-1

Book Four—*Sarah Jane: Liberty's Torch*
ISBN-10: 0-9753036-9-4
ISBN-13: 978-0-9753036-9-6

Book Five—*Eleanor Jo: The Farmer's Daughter*
ISBN-10: 0-9788726-1-4
ISBN-13: 978-0-9788726-1-8

Book Six—*Melanie Ann: A Legacy of Love*
ISBN-10: 0-9788726-2-2
ISBN-13: 978-0-9788726-2-5

Visit our Web site at: www.eleanorseries.com

About the
Author

*E*LEANOR CLARK LIVES IN central Texas with Lee, her husband of over 50 years, and as maternal patriarch of the family, she is devoted to her 5 children, 17 grandchildren, and 4 great grandchildren.

Born the daughter of a Texas sharecropper and raised in the Great Depression, Eleanor was a female pioneer in crossing economic, gender, educational, and corporate barriers. An executive for one of America's most prestigious ministries, Eleanor later founded her own highly successful consulting firm. Her appreciation of her American and Christian heritage comes to life along with her exciting and colorful family history in the youth fiction series, *The Eleanor Series*.